THE
BOY
WHO
CLIMBED
INTO
THE
MOON

Other books by David Almond

Skellig

Kit's Wilderness

Heaven Eyes

Counting Stars

Secret Heart

Wild Girl, Wild Boy – A Play

Skellig – A Play

The Fire-Eaters

Clay

My Dad's A Birdman

The Savage

Jackdaw Summer

THE BOY WHO CLIMBED INTO THE MOON

DAVID ALMOND

illustrated by
POLLY DUNBAR

WALKER
BOOKS

First published 2010 by Walker Books Ltd
87 Vauxhall Walk, London SE11 5HJ

2 4 6 8 10 9 7 5 3 1

Text © 2010 David Almond
Illustrations © 2010 Polly Dunbar

The right of David Almond and Polly Dunbar to be identified
as author and illustrator respectively of this work has been
asserted by them in accordance with the Copyright,
Designs and Patents Act 1988

This book has been typeset in Plantin

Printed in China

British Library Cataloguing in Publication Data:
a catalogue record for this book is available
from the British Library

ISBN 978-1-4063-1457-1

www.walker.co.uk

For Tod, June, Hana,
and especially Noa
D. A.

For Oliver
P. D.

1

Some time ago, there was a rather lonely boy named Paul who lived in a city in the north of England. He lived underground, in a basement flat at the bottom of a great apartment block. Over his head, there was floor after floor after floor, and family after family.

This made the world seem very heavy and the sky seem very far away.

One day, Paul was absent from school. He said he had a headache and a stomach ache. He said he felt as if he was going down with a bug or the flu or a fever. But he knew, and his mum and his dad knew, that there was really not much wrong at all. He simply didn't like school, and school didn't seem to like him. He was pleased that his parents understood this, and that on rare days like today they allowed him to stay at home.

Paul wondered what he should do with his day. He heard his dad getting ready for work. He heard his mum singing in the shower. He stared at the walls of the basement flat. He realized that he had no idea what to do, and he also realized, to his great surprise, that he felt quite bored.

Oh, dear, he thought. *What on earth shall I do?*

Amazingly, he knew the answer straight away.

"I shall go and touch the sky," he said.

This was very strange, for nobody, least of all Paul himself, had ever thought that he might be adventurous.

He slipped out of the basement flat, went through the door of the apartment block, and started to climb.

The stairs were steep. There was stairway after stairway. There were signs that said:

FLOOR 1
FLOOR 2
FLOOR 3
FLOOR 4
FLOOR 5
FLOOR 6

His footsteps rang out and echoed off the walls as he climbed. He heard chattering from the families in the apartments. He smelt sausages being cooked. He licked his lips. He imagined the lovely taste of sausages on his tongue.

At Floor 9, a young man wearing shorts and trainers and a vest with HARRIER written on it, came leaping down the stairs. He halted and looked at Paul. He pressed a button on the stopwatch on his wrist.

"Good morning, young man!" said the young man.

Paul looked down. He wasn't very good at speaking to strangers.

"And where might you be off to?" said the young man.

Paul said nothing.

"Come along," said the young man. "I haven't got all day. There's jogging and running and sprinting to do."

"I'm going to the top," murmured Paul.

"What did you say?" said the young man. He kept jogging on the spot and rocking his shoulders and lifting his knees high.

"I'm going to the top to touch the sky," said Paul, a little louder.

"Excellent!" said the young man. "My name is Harry! And you?"

"I'm Paul," said Paul.

"Excellent! You realize that you could take the lift, of course," said Harry. "Just like everybody else does."

Paul just looked at him. He hadn't thought there might be a lift.

"But you're not like everybody else, are you?" said Harry. "You never take the lift, do you? You're a harrier just like me." He jogged faster and faster and his knees and elbows thrashed the air until they could hardly be seen, and his hair swung wildly around his head. "You like to keep fit. Don't you, Paul?"

Paul looked at Harry. He tried to imagine wearing running shoes and a vest with HARRIER written on it and jogging on the spot until his knees disappeared and wearing a stopwatch on his wrist.

"Yes," said Paul.

"Good for you!" said Harry. "Onwards and upwards, that's what I say!"

He grinned. He pressed a button on his stopwatch.

"Farewell, young man!" he said. "And give my love to Mabel."

"Who's Mabel?" said Paul, but Harry was off again, bounding down the stairs. Paul listened to his footsteps fading into the distance far below. Then he went through a door that said **FLOOR 9** to find the lift, and there it was.

The buttons for the lift were on the wall. Of course the button for the top floor, which was Floor 29, was at the very top. Paul jumped and jumped to try to reach it. He was about to give up and climb the stairs again when a hand reached over his head and pressed the button for him. The hand belonged to a lady wearing a red coat and red spectacles and carrying a white poodle on her arm. The poodle was wearing a red coat. The lady peered through her red spectacles.

"I see you're going to the top," she said.

"Yes," said Paul. "Floor 29. I'm going to touch the sky."

"Excellent!" said the lady. "You must be Mabel's nephew, then."

She put out her hand. Paul looked at it for a moment, then he decided he should shake it.

"Very pleased to meet you," said the lady.

"My name is Clara. Mabel has often talked to us about you. Hasn't she, Clarence?"

"Yap!" said the dog.

"You're smaller than we thought," said Clara. "Isn't he, Clarence?"

"Yap!" said the dog.

Paul stared at them.

"What's my name?" said Paul.

"Your name?" said Clara. "Let me think. Help me, Clarence."

"Yap!" said the dog.

"No, it wasn't that," said Clara.

"It's Paul," said Paul.

"Of course it is!" said Clara. "How could we forget?"

The lift arrived and the door opened.

"Off you go, then, Paul," said Clara.

Paul stepped inside.

"Give our love to Mabel," said Clara.

"Yap!" said the dog.

The doors closed and the lift began to rise towards the top. As it rose, Paul thought of the sky outside getting emptier and emptier and bluer and bluer. He thought of all the families and apartments below. Then the lift stopped and the doors opened and he stepped out onto Floor 29.

2

There was a landing with doors to the apartments. There were lots of flowers in vases and pots. A great big window looked out over the city in the north. Paul saw the networks of streets, and cars and buses and lorries. He saw tiny people scurrying to and fro. He saw birds flying and wheeling below him. He saw the city stretching all around him, and then the fields and hills and

woods that lay beyond, and
then distant hazy mountains,
then places where he couldn't
tell where the earth ended and
the sky began.

He shivered with excitement.
This was like something from one of
his very best dreams. He pressed his
face and hands to the cold glass and he
imagined reaching through it to touch
the sky.

"Goodness gracious!" someone squeaked.

Paul spun around. An apartment door was open and a little woman stood there.

"It's a boy!" she squeaked.

Paul took a deep breath. *Be brave*, he told himself.

"Hello, Mabel," said Paul.

The woman frowned.

"Don't you Mabel me, lad!" she said. "What are you doing here?"

"Looking at the sky," said Paul. "I'd like to touch it. Harry sends his love. And so do Clara and Clarence."

At that moment they heard fast footsteps on the stairs.

"Perhaps that's Harry now," said Paul.

They heard the lift coming.

"And perhaps that's Clara and Clarence," said Paul.

The door to the stairs burst open and Paul's dad ran out, gasping for breath. The lift door opened and Paul's mum stepped out with her eyes wide in fright.

"Paul!" they yelled. "What are you doing here?"

They ran to him and hugged him tight. They sobbed and sobbed and hugged and hugged. Paul's mum said a woman in red had told her where

he'd gone. Paul's dad said a harrier had told him where he'd gone. They said they were frantic, they were terrified.

"How could you think of doing such a thing?" they cried.

Paul didn't know the answer. He wasn't sure that he'd even thought about it at all.

He looked at Mabel. Mabel looked at him.

"This is Mabel," said Paul.

"No, it's not," said Mabel.

"But Clara and Harry said—"

"Clara and Harry! They're way behind the times. I changed my name this very morning to Molly. A much nicer name don't you think? Well, don't you?"

Paul and his mum and dad looked at each other.

"Yes," said Paul's mum at last.

"Of course it is," said Molly. "But of course I still look like Mabel. So I will tell people that I am Mabel's identical twin sister. I will say that Mabel is on holiday in Barbados, and I have come to look after her apartment while she is away. Shall we try it?"

"Try what?" said Paul's dad.

"Try asking me where Mabel is," said Molly. "Go on, don't be shy."

"Where is Mabel?" asked Paul's dad.

"Oh," said Molly. "She has gone on holiday to Barbados. I am her identical twin sister, Molly. I am looking after her apartment while she is away."

"That's nice," said Paul's dad.

Molly smiled.

"See?" she said. "It works. Now, why don't you all come inside?"

23

18

22

20

19

3

The walls of Molly's apartment

were filled with great big numbers and with paintings of people arranged around them. Paul saw paintings of Harry in his jogging gear and of Clara holding Clarence.

They're just like real life! he thought to himself.

"Mabel is an artist," said Molly. "These are paintings of the people who live in the apartment block. They are arranged floor by floor. And look, there is the lady herself. It is her self-portrait."

She pointed to a figure standing beside the number 29.

26

25

29

28

27

"See how closely she resembles me?" said Molly.

"Yes," said Paul.

"Good," said Molly. "Identical, just as I said. Now, you said you wished to touch the sky."

"Yes," said Paul.

"A fine ambition for a boy. Come with me."

She took his hand and led him to the window. There was a pigeon on the ledge outside, looking in with beady eyes.

"Shoo!" said Molly, and the pigeon flapped away.

Then she turned a handle in the window frame and pulled, and the window rose, ever so slightly. There was just a thin band of sky between the window and its frame.

"It will not open any further," said Molly. "Perhaps they are worried that people in the high apartments will fly away. But put your hands through. Touch the sky."

Paul took a deep breath. He breathed in the draught of sky that flowed into the room. He slid the fingers of his right hand through the gap. He waggled them. He touched the sky.

"Can you feel it?" said Molly.

"Yes," whispered Paul.

"What does it feel like?"

"It feels cold ... and fresh ... and blue ... and sweet ... and fizzy ... and flappy." He gazed through the window to his hand waggling outside. "It feels magnificent!"

Everyone laughed and smiled.

"Go on," said Molly. "Touch it with your left hand, too."

So he did, and with two handfuls of fingers waggling out there, it felt even more magnificent. He leaned right against the glass. He reached further and out went his wrists, out went his forearms right to his elbow. He sighed and giggled at the feel of the sky against his skin.

Molly pointed up at her ceiling.

"If you look closely," she said, "you will see that there is a trapdoor."

They all looked. Yes, there was a rectangular shape cut into the ceiling.

"There are rumours," said Molly, "that it leads directly to the roof. Or so I have been told by Mabel."

"But wouldn't that be dangerous?" said Paul's mum.

"I have no idea," said Molly.

Paul looked at the trapdoor, and thought about the roof, and about how it would be even more magnificent out there.

"Now," said Molly. "I believe that boys enjoy sausages. Am I correct?"

"Yes," said Paul.

"Good," said Molly. "And parents like to take tea and cakes. Sit down and I will feed you."

Paul sat at a round table beside the window with his parents. The worry and fright slowly faded from their faces. Molly put some sausages into a frying pan. She switched on a kettle and cut into a cherry cake. The pigeon perched on the window ledge again and peered in with beady eyes.

"Mabel is painting downwards floor by floor," said Molly. "She has reached floor number 17. It is her ambition to paint the whole apartment block." She lowered her voice. "If truth be told, it is her ambition to paint the whole *world*. Of course there will never be enough time for that. Where do you live?"

"In the basement," said Paul's dad.

"Aha! Underground!" said Molly. "She will reach you eventually."

Paul's dad winked. "Once she has returned from Barbados," he said.

"Correct," said Molly. "Once she has returned."

She put the cake and the sausages and some cups of tea and a glass of lemonade and a big bottle of tomato ketchup onto the table.

They ate and drank. Molly held her fingers together like a frame and looked through it at them.

"If *I* were a painter," she said, "I could make a very attractive portrait of you all. But that, of course, is Mabel's job."

"So what is *your* job?" said Paul's mum.

"I am…" said Mabel, "a polar explorer."

"How fascinating!" said Paul's dad. "North or South?"

"Sorry?" replied Mabel.

"North Pole or South Pole?"

"The other one," said Mabel.

"I didn't know there was another one."

"Of course you didn't. It is still largely unexplored."

She stroked her nose and wondered deeply for a while.

"Maybe we should go now," whispered Paul's mum. "Come along."

But Molly suddenly said, "Have you met my brother?"

"Your brother?" said Paul's dad.

"He's an odd and clever man," said Molly. "He has the strangest ideas. Come and see!"

She picked up a telescope from the corner of the room and went to the window. She angled the telescope towards the earth and stared through it.

"Yes!" she said. "There he is, hard at work as usual."

She held out the telescope to Paul.

"Down there!" she said. Paul looked through the telescope. He saw streets and houses and cars. "Do you see him?" said Molly.

"No," said Paul. "To be honest, I'm not quite sure what I'm looking for."

"What do you mean, *to be honest*? And what do you mean, *not quite sure what you're looking for*? You're looking for my brother!" She pursed her lips. "Have you imagined him yet?"

Paul said nothing.

"You haven't, have you?" said Molly. "Goodness gracious! How can you see him if you haven't imagined him first? You will see him working with wood, in his garden, as usual. It is very simple. Now. Look again!"

Paul looked at his mum and dad. They shrugged. He imagined a man working with wood in a garden, then he looked through the telescope again and he gasped with surprise. There, far below, was a little curly-haired man working in a little garden outside a little shed. He had a saw in his hand.

"Well?" said Molly.

"Yes," said Paul. He kept on looking. It was very strange.

"Excellent! His name is Benjamin."

She took the telescope away from Paul.

"Now," she said, "just one more thing. Do you have strange ideas, too?"

Paul looked at his mum and dad again. He didn't know what to say.

"Well?" said Molly. "Come along! Yes or no? And if it's yes, give me one strange idea and then we'll know what's what."

"Well…" said Paul.

Molly rolled her eyes. She impatiently tapped her toe on the floor.

Paul looked out of the window. A strange idea? He had been told at school that he had no ideas at all, never mind strange ones. He had been told by one teacher that he was an empty-headed buffoon. But he looked Molly in the eye. He might as well say something.

"Well…" he said again. "Sometimes…"

"Sometimes what?" snapped Molly.

"Sometimes I think the moon is not the moon, but is a hole in the sky and…"

Molly clapped her hands.

"Excellent! That's just the kind of thing we need to know!"

She turned to Paul's dad.

"What do you do?" she said.

"Do?" said Paul's dad.

"What job do you do? I am a polar explorer. You…"

"I drive a taxi," said Paul's dad.

"I thought you would! That's how we'll get there. Come along. We're off to see my brother! Taxi!"

4

At the lift door, Paul's mum tapped him on the shoulder.

"I didn't know you thought that," she said.

"Thought what?" said Paul.

"Thought that the moon was a hole in the sky, of course."

Paul thought about it.

"Neither did I," he said. "At least, I didn't know I thought it till I said it."

The lift hummed to a halt and the doors opened before them. They stepped inside. There was a man sitting on a stool. He had a peaked helmet on his head and a clipboard and pencil in his hands.

"Good morning!" he announced. "May I ask—?"

"No, Tom!" said Molly. "Absolutely not!"

She turned her face away from him.

"Take no notice of him!" she told the others.

The man's face fell. Off they went, downwards, downwards.

Molly pressed button number 9 and the lift stopped at floor number 9. The doors opened and there was Clara in her red coat and Clarence in his.

"Good afternoon, Mabel," said Clara.

"I have stopped to inform you that I am not Mabel," said Molly. "Mabel is on holiday in Moscow. I am her identical twin sister, Molly. Very pleased to meet you."

She reached out of the lift and shook Clara's hand.

"Pleased to meet you, too," said Clara. "This is Clarence. I see you have your nephew with you."

"Yes," said Molly. "He is a boy with strange ideas."

"Aha!" said Clara. "Clarence has those, too."

"Such as?" said Molly.

"Such as," said Clara, "he thinks that when he grows to seven years old, a poodle, if he has lived well, will achieve the power of flight and the power of speech."

"Excellent!" said Molly. "And has he lived well?"

"Yap!" said the dog.

"He has indeed," said Clara. "His life has been exemplary."

Clarence looked very pleased with himself.

The doors closed.

"Hang on a moment," said Paul's dad. "You told Clara that your sister is in Moscow. I thought she was meant to be in Barbados."

"That's correct!" said Molly. "Moscow is now part of Barbados. It is to do with environmental changes and tectonic plates."

Down they went. Downwards, downwards. The lift hummed to a halt and out they stepped.

"Farewell," mumbled the man in the helmet.

"Farewell, Tom," said Molly. "Thank you for your silence."

As the lift doors closed, Harry sprinted out from the stairwell.

"Caught you!" he said to Paul. "Using the lift, eh? I'm disappointed in you, lad! You'll be a lump of lard before you can say sausage sandwich."

He bounced away into the street outside.

"Sausage sandwich," whispered Paul, but he stayed just the same.

They stepped through the door of the apartment block. Paul's mum pointed down to the basement flat and said that was where they lived. Everyone looked down. Molly said that it was very far away but that it looked very cosy.

Paul thought about Clarence the poodle.

"How old is Clarence?" said Paul.

"Let me see," said Molly. "He must be six years, eleven months, three weeks and six days. Now, where's that taxi? Taxi!"

5

Paul's dad's taxi was green with a bright red stripe and a sign at the top that said:

TAKE A TIP TOP TAXI
TO THE VERY VERY TOP

Molly sat in the front with Paul's dad, Paul in the back with his mum.

"Off we go!" said Molly. "Straight ahead for 732 yards, then third left, and second left when you see a black-and-white cat."

Paul's dad did as he was told, then slowed down.

"But there's no black-and-white cat," he said.

"Of course there is!" said Molly. "Mrs Wiffen on Floor 10 has two of them! Oh, this will do! Left here, then quickly left again."

Paul's dad did as he was told. They came back into the street they'd started from.

"This is where we started from!" said Paul's dad.

"Of course it's not," said Molly. "Did you see that man in the green hat last time we were here?"

"No," said Paul's dad.

"Well, then," said Molly. "So how can it be the same place? Now, left, left, left and left again, then right, right, right and right again."

The taxi rocked and rolled and lurched left and right. The apartment block kept looming in and out of sight. Paul's dad kept saying they were in the same silly street. Molly kept saying of course they weren't.

"Just follow my directions, man," she said. "Do you think I don't know the way to my own brother's?

Left,

left,

left,

left;

         right,

         right,

         right,

         right;

left,

left,

left,

left;

         right,

         right,

         right,

         right."

In the back of the car, Paul's mum whispered, "What did Clara mean?"

"About what?" said Paul.

"About you being Molly's nephew."

"She has me confused with somebody else," said Paul.

"With who?" said his mum.

"With Mabel's nephew."

"How come?" said his mum.

"I haven't a clue," said Paul.

"That's it!" said Molly. "Look, a man carrying a brown briefcase! Now, all we need to see is a girl eating a burger and we're nearly there."

They all looked out.

"There," said Paul. "A girl eating a burger!"

"Is she blonde and does she have fries?" said Molly.

"Yes!" said Paul.

"Excellent!" said Molly. "Then this is the right street! Now, left then right and straight ahead and stop under the tree."

Paul's dad drove into a street lined with hundreds of trees. He slowed down and looked at Molly.

"Which tree?" he sighed.

"Which tree? The one outside my brother's house, of course!" said Molly.

Paul's dad sighed again. He drove along the street and stopped.

"Excellent!" said Molly. "You must have been here before!"

And out she jumped.

6

"Now," said Molly. "Some background. My brother used to be very very very shy. So shy that he hardly spoke at all. So shy that he spent the first twenty years of his life with a brown paper bag on his head. By the time he took it off at last, he had a full beard and he was so pale and handsome and dewy-eyed that our mother spent her time chasing away the girls with buckets of water. A film director came and wanted him to be a star. A bishop came and wanted him to be a saint. He was just about to put the paper bag back on when the army came and took him off to war."

"To war?" said Paul's dad. "Which war?"

"The last one," said Molly. "You know, that noisy one with all the bullets and bombs and explosions. The War of the Thingummyjig or the Whatdyacallit or the Great Big Ginormous War Number 9. Maybe you missed it. Maybe you were away. Maybe it was before your time. Anyway, all the noises and running about and all the fright left him rather strange. Often he is very sad, but on his good days he is very keen and active, and when his brain can be unscrambled it contains a multitude of ideas that could be the salvation of us all. Now, come along, follow me. And let's hope it's one of his good days."

She opened a gate and led them towards a little terraced house with a green door. Beside the door, there was a little arched alleyway. She led them through.

"Benjamin!" she called softly. "Coooeee! Oh, Benjamin!"

Beyond the alleyway, there were massive bean plants, giant sunflowers, and huge hollyhocks. There were bees buzzing and birds tweeting and swooping. There was a thin path of old bricks that led them deeper and deeper into the foliage.

"But the garden I saw was titchy," said Paul.

"Titchy!" said Molly. "That was from way up high, and far away, and the traffic was busy, and the pigeon was in the way, and anyway the whole point of a garden is that it grows... And anyway anyway, which end of the telescope did you look through?"

"The right end," said Paul.

"There you are, then. You were supposed to look through the left!" Then she stopped. "There! At last! Benjamin! It's me, your sister Molly!"

There was a small square lawn covered in sawdust and curly wood shavings bordered by magnolias. There was a wooden workbench with a saw and chisels on it. There were wooden models of animals and people. There was a little wooden shed with the door half-open.

They crept closer. Molly slowly pulled the door.

"Benjamin," Molly whispered. "Benjamin?"

Paul and his mum and dad peered over Molly's shoulder. A man sat dead still in an ancient armchair. He had green overalls on and a sack over his head. There were black words stamped on the sack:

BEST
JERUSALEM
ARTICHOKES

"Oh, dear," whispered Molly. "A relapse."

She opened the door wide.

"It's your sister Molly," she hissed. "I can see you, Benjamin."

She stepped forwards. She lifted the sack off his head and there he was, gazing into the light with his beard and his pale skin and his dewy eyes. He was very, very glum, and there were tears in the corners of his eyes.

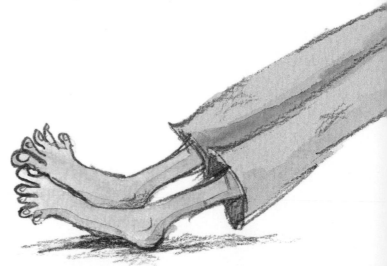

"I have brought some people to meet you," said Molly, "including a child with some very peculiar ideas. Say hello."

Benjamin sadly turned his eyes to them all, but said nothing.

"Stand up, dear," said Molly. "And come and have a chat."

He did as he was told. He was tall and thin and he had to stoop through the door to get into the garden.

"But you were little and curly!" said Paul.

Benjamin made no reply.

They sat on the lawn. It was warm and soft. There was a pear tree over them, with tiny new pears hanging there. The sun was slowly travelling through the sky and the shadow of the apartment block inched towards them.

"Now, then," said Molly. "How are you today?"

He said nothing.

"How *happy* are you?" she said.

He sighed.

"On a scale of one to ten?" said Benjamin. His voice was very slow and very low.

"Yes, if you like," said Molly.

"Which is happy?" he said. "Is it number one or number ten?"

Molly pondered.

"Happy is ten!" she said at last.

"Ohhhhh," he groaned. "Then I am the glummest of the glum, for I am one."

"Oh, poor, poor soul," said Paul's mum, and Benjamin looked at her and nodded and the tears rolled down his face and splashed down onto the grass.

"Hang on!" snapped Molly. "Silly me! I was wrong, Benjamin. Forgive me. Happy is number one!"

"Really?" said Benjamin.

"Really really really!" answered Molly.

A great transformation took place upon his face.

"Gadzooks!" he said. "Then if I'm number one, it means I am happy!"

"Correct!" said Molly. "In fact, you couldn't possibly be happier!"

Benjamin clenched his fists and punched the air. He stood up and danced a jig.

"Yippeee!" he yelled. "I feel so ... oh, magnificent! I haven't felt better since tea time three weeks gone last March! Oh, joy!
Yippeeeeeeeeee!"

"Excellent!" said Molly. "Now, calm down and say hello to these good people."

He did one more twirl, one more twist, gave

one more yippee and said, "Good afternoon, you lovely people." He leaned down towards Paul. "You must be the one with the ideas. Very good to meet you, boy! We'll have to chew some fat and get some crackpot notions going. Yes! Happiness! Happiness at last!"

"But you were little," said Paul when Benjamin began to calm down. "And you had curly hair, and…"

"Ah, that was long ago," said Benjamin. "You have to keep up with things."

"But it was just an hour ago," said Paul.

"An hour!" said Benjamin. "A lot can happen in a second, never mind an hour. Look what's just happened to me. And think of Pluto."

"Pluto?"

"The planet. Once we had no idea it was there at all. Then Vladimir Whatsit looks up through his telescope and there it is. One minute, nothing, emptiness, blackness, vastness, silence; the next, bingo! Pluto, there she is sailing through the heavens."

"But—" said Paul.

"And now," continued Benjamin, "they have decided that Pluto has never been there at all. From nothingness to existence and straight back to nothingness again – all in two blinks of an eye."

"But—" said Paul.

"But nothing," said Benjamin. "That is the longest speech I have made in a year. Enough!" And he shut his mouth tight and goggled at Paul. "Yyyyr trrrn t ay u-in," he mumbled.

"What?" said Paul.

"He says it's your turn to say something," said Molly. "It is his conversational method."

"What will I say?" said Paul.

"Anything you like."

"Go on, love," said Paul's mum.

"Don't be shy," said his dad.

Paul pondered.

"It's a lovely day," he said.

Benjamin clicked his tongue.

"Orrrrr-nggggg," he mumbled.

"He says that's boring," said Molly.

Paul looked down. A black beetle skittered past his foot. Then he stared into the sky. A crow flapped over him. Boring. He'd always worried that he might be boring. Maybe it'd be best if he just went home. Maybe it'd be better if he was back in school.

"U aong!" said Benjamin.

"Come along," said Molly.

"I u oan ay uthin a I u a hack o y ed a e," said Benjamin.

"If you don't say something fast I'll put the sack on my head again," translated Molly. She poked Paul in the chest.

"Do it!" she said. "Tell him what you told me. About the moon!"

"But that was just—"

"Try it! You might as well if you've got nothing else to say."

Paul licked his lips.

"Sometimes..." he started.

Benjamin leaned forwards and widened his eyes and rested his chin on his hand and nodded and waited.

Paul licked his lips again. He sighed.

"Sometimes," he said, and he looked down and he felt his face burning. "Sometimes I think... Sometimes I think the moon is not the moon but is a hole in the sky."

Benjamin pondered.

"An interesting theory," he said.

"It's not a theory," said Paul. "It just popped out of my mouth when I didn't expect it to."

"But that's the very best kind of theory!" said Benjamin. "No planning, no warnings, just bingo – a theory that changes the world! And this one could explain a lot!"

"Like what?" said Paul's dad.

"Ah," said Benjamin, and a tear popped out and rolled like a slow theory from the corner of his eye. "To explain that, I must take you back in time. I must take you to a time of war." He reached up and shook a branch that hung over them, and fat yellow pears tumbled through the air and settled on the grass all around them. Paul and his mum and his dad looked at them in astonishment. They each bit into one and each one was perfectly ripe and sweet and juicy. Paul's dad was about to speak about this, but Benjamin held up his hand for silence.

"Now," he said, "eat some fruit, my good people, and I will take you back in time."

7

"It was whiz bang wallop,

it was bing bang boom," said Benjamin. "It was crash flash smash. It was noise and heat and pain and howls and buildings toppling and fires burning and flashing light all through the night and black clouds swirling round all day. And on it went and on and on and on and on and on and on, day after day after day after day, week after week after week after week, and… This is a long speech, too. You've loosened my tongue, lad, and it's about to tell a tale that starts in deepest grimness and ends in highest hope."

He shook his head and a single tear dropped from each eye.

"War," he said. "What good's war? How can there be any other answer but no blinking good at all?" He looked Paul in the eye. "You got any other answer, son?"

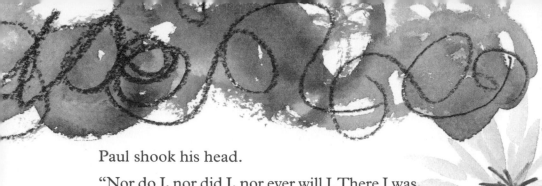

Paul shook his head.

"Nor do I, nor did I, nor ever will I. There I was, a feller that'd spent his life with a sack on his head. And they came to me and they said if you take that sack off and shave that beard off and shave that head and toughen up, you'll have an exciting life, my lad. So I said, 'That sounds like fun. That sounds like just the kind of thing I've been missing.' Why did I believe them? Because, my lad, I knew nothing better! Do you know anything better, lad?"

"Better than what?" said Paul.

"Goodness gracious! Better than going to war, of course!" said Benjamin.

Paul pondered. He'd never really thought about it, but surely everything was better than going to war.

"U o!" groaned Benjamin.

"Come on!" said Molly.

"Ee u!"

"Speak up!"

"Sausages," said Paul. He looked Benjamin in the eye. He was getting better at this, better and bolder. "Eating sausages," he declared, "is much better than going to war."

"Brilliant!" said Benjamin. He looked at Paul's parents. "I hope you know how proud of this boy you should be," he said.

"We do," whispered Paul's mum.

"Excellent!" said Benjamin. "Anyway, there I was at war..." Then he paused and leaned his face close to Paul. "You're not contemplating becoming a politician, are you?" he said.

Paul blinked. This was something else he hadn't really considered until now.

"You should," said Benjamin. "We could do with a prime minister with your wisdom. Every time a war threatens – get sausage production into overdrive now! Ha! You're a lad after my own heart. Here, have a pear!" He breathed deeply and sadly. "Trouble was, in our war, there wasn't a sausage in sight. So I had to find my own solution."

"What was that?" said Paul.

"I died."

"You *died*?" said Paul's dad.

"Correct! It was the obvious solution. There we were, billions and zillions of us lined up on the battlefield, armed to the teeth, glaring and growling and gnashing our teeth, all of us determined to kill as many of each other as we possibly could. I just took a short cut. Soon as any battle started, I just dropped down dead."

He took a bite of his pear, licked the juice from his lips and gazed at the others. Molly reached out and tenderly stroked his arm.

"*Really*?" said Paul.

"Really. Soon as I heard the first bullet, down I went, every time."

"But you're not…" said Paul's mum.

"I know," said Benjamin. He contemplated the sky. "And I have to admit," he continued, "that sometimes I find it rather confusing myself. I dropped down dead at the start, knew nothing for a while, then when it was all over I came to life again. Quite pleasant, really. Quite restful. And of course it brought the war to an end, so there's that in its favour."

Paul's dad peered at Benjamin. What on earth did he mean?

"What on earth do you mean?" he said.

Benjamin sighed. A tear fell from his eye.

"Oh, dear. See how quickly we forget the lessons of our history," he said. "It brought about the end because it was catching. It became an epidemic. First there was just a handful of us falling down at the first bullet. Before long it was a platoon, then a cohort, then a brigade, then… On the last day, the big fat general with the big fat medals gave the order to attack and the whole army dropped like stones into the grass."

"*Really*?" said Paul.

"Really," said Benjamin. "Read the history books. Of course, I think some of us were just pretending to be dead, but does that matter?"

"No," said Paul.

"Course not. And of course the odd thing was it had all been happening on the other side as well. An epidemic of dying and death and dropping at the crack of the first bullet. And can the dead fight each other?"

Paul and the others shook their heads.

"Correct," said Benjamin. "They cannot. And would the generals fight each other? They would not. So that was the end of that. A few hours of silence and peace and the dead start getting up and heading home. I came back to the garden. Been here ever since. All alone, except for visitations from my sister… What did you say your name was?"

"Molly," said Molly.

"Ah, yes," said Benjamin. "So you did, Molly." He peered at her then shrugged and smiled. "And to think I used to think I understood a thing or two."

He bit into another pear.

"Excuse me," said Paul, getting braver all the time. "But what's that all got to do with the moon?"

"The moon?" said Benjamin. "Absolutely nothing at all!"

"But my theory," said Paul. "You said it was—"

"And so it was!"

Then Benjamin slapped his brow.

"Oh, I see!" he exclaimed. "Of course! We do that thing where you propose a theory and I support it or refute it with a suggestion of my own. Which was I about to do?"

"You were about to support it, dear," said Molly.

"Aha!" said Benjamin. "To explain that, I must take you back in time. I must take you to a time of war."

"You've already done that," said Molly.

"Have I? Oh, yes. Well, then, no preambles – straight to the battlefield! There I was, lying dead in a ditch, watching the wide sky above me and rockets flying and planes whizzing and missiles—"

"You saw them?" said Paul. "But I thought you said you were dead."

Benjamin pursed his lips.

"This is a bright boy," he mused. "Now listen, in the attempt to explain the inexplicable, I will take a short diversion. First of all, a question! Have you ever felt, as you are walking along the street, that you are being watched?"

Paul pondered. He tried to remember. He had to admit to himself that he did not often walk along a street.

"Ee u!" muttered Benjamin.

"Speak up," said Molly.

"Aye i ayin."

"Time is flying!"

"I suppose so," said Paul, though he wasn't certain.

"That's the dead!" said Benjamin. "They're watching all the time. Just like I was watching when I lay in the ditch. Oh, and if you feel itchy when you think you're being watched, it's a cat."

"A *cat*?" said Paul's mum.

"Yes," said Benjamin. "A dead cat. It's the fleas. They like to jump back to the land of the living. Anyway, there I was, dead in a ditch, and it's all pretty comfortable and the day's coming to an end and the booming's not so boomy and the banging's not so bangy and the battle's nearly done and here's the moon starting to shine and I see it."

"It?"

"It. A bomber. A black pointy wingy thing curving through the evening sky. Quite lovely, too. Quite elegant. Strange how doomy things like that can be so lovely, too. Maybe that's why we're so attached to them, eh? Anyway, there it is, curving

through the sky with a lovely stream of fire at its tail, and as it's passing straight towards the face of the moon, I think, *That's coming for you, Benjamin. That's absolutely definitely heading for your ditch.* And I can see that others think that, too, because there's such a screeching and panicking and scarpering all around and soldiers running like rabbits away from where I am. Then suddenly, it's gone. Bang! Or should I say, not bang! No more pointy wingy thing. Gone."

"How's that?" said Paul's dad.

"Not out!" said Benjamin. He giggled. "Sorry. It was the moon. The bomber went straight into the moon. And I thought to myself, as I came back from being dead, *That thing up there is not the moon. It is in fact a great big hole in the sky.* So there we are, lad. Support for your proposition." He rubbed his hands with glee. "But what we need is proof!"

He scratched his head. He looked at Paul's dad. He leaned close to him and peered into his eyes.

"May I ask you a question, sir?" he said.

"Of course," said Paul's dad.

Benjamin rubbed his chin.

"Think carefully before you answer," he said. "What, apart from driving taxis, do you actually do?"

"Do?"

"Do."

"I'm also a window cleaner," said Paul's dad.

Benjamin clapped his hands.

"I knew it! Soon as I saw you, I said there's a man with a head for heights! What's your name, by the way?"

"Alfred," said Paul's dad.

"A very sensible name. Now then, Alfred, another question. Am I right to assume that you use ladders in the course of your work?"

"You are," said Alfred.

"Excellent! And where might these ladders be found?"

"In the lock-up," said Alfred.

"Aha, the lock-up! And where might this lock-up be found, Alfred?"

"It's just behind the apartment block."

"Aha!" Benjamin tapped his cheek. "Now, think carefully. Take your time. Which apartment block?"

Alfred turned and pointed into the sky, at the great big shadowed building that loomed so close to them.

"That one there," he said.

"Gadzooks!" said Benjamin. "Where on earth did that come from?"

And he leapt to his feet and sprinted for the exit from the garden, yelling, "No time to waste! Alfred's ladders will change the course of human history! Follow me! Taxi!"

8

But he stopped at the gate. He
started to shake.

"But-but..." he stammered.

"But what?" said Molly.

"But-but I've not been out since the war! I
need my s-sack!"

"Your sack?"

"I see too much! And the world can see too
much of me!"

"Be brave!" said Molly.

"Be bold!" said Paul.

"That's what they s-s-said in the war!" said
Benjamin. "That's when I dropped down d-dead!
Oh, golly, I've got the willies!"

Tears ran down his cheeks. He closed his eyes.
He started to sway. He started to topple. Paul
reached out. He held Benjamin's arm.

"You're safe with me," he murmured.

"Am I?" said Benjamin.

"Yes. Lean on me."

Benjamin sighed.

"We were meant to meet," he whispered. "We're
each other's destiny."

He let Paul guide him to the door of the taxi. They squeezed into the back with Molly.

"This time I'll follow my own route," said Alfred.

"Suit yourself," said Molly.

He drove straight out of Benjamin's street, straight across a main road and straight to the apartment block.

"See?" he said. "Two minutes flat!"

"Huh!" said Molly. "That's a line, not a route. Much more boring and much less scenic. Anyway, everybody knows that it always *seems* to take longer to get to a place than to get back again. And anyway *anyway,* it's time to stop blathering. Just get the lock-up unlocked and find that silly ladder."

"Please don't be rude to my dad," said Paul.

"What did you say?" said Molly.

Paul gulped. He hadn't spoken like this in his life. He took a deep breath.

"I said," he said, "do not be rude to my dad."

Molly took a deep breath of her own. She was about to speak again.

"Paul's right," said his mum. "Say you're sorry, Molly. And Alfred, tell Molly it's all right."

"Sorry," said Molly.

"It's all right," said Alfred.

"Gadzooks," said Benjamin. "I begin to see

where the boy gets his wisdom from. What might your name be, madam?"

"It *might* be Rasputin," said Paul's mum. "But it is not. It is Francesca."

"A fine name," said Benjamin. "Now, to the lock-up and on with the quest!"

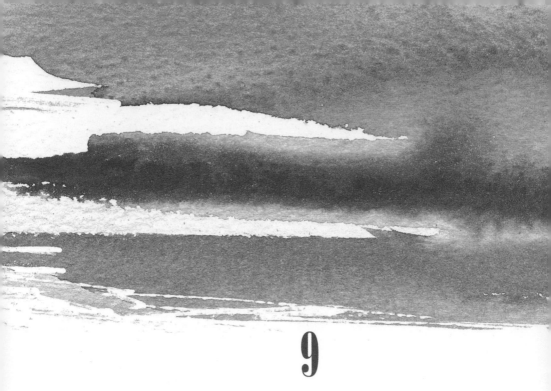

9

The sky was darkening. Great glorious streaks of red and gold hung over the city. Lights glowed in the windows of the apartment block. Alfred led the others along a rectangular pathway to a line of garages. He unlocked one and took out an aluminium ladder. It was made of three sections all gleaming and glittering where they caught the light.

"A ladder fit for the gods!" exclaimed Benjamin. "Where on earth did you obtain such a thing?"

"B&Q," said Alfred. "£54.99."

He hoisted the ladder to his shoulders.

"What's the plan?" he asked.

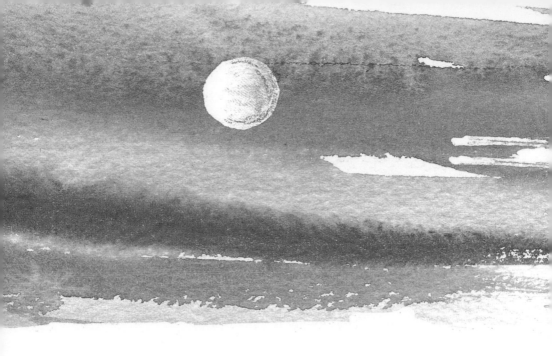

"The *plan*?" said Benjamin. "What could be more boring than a plan? How can we plan when the outcome is unknown? How can we plan for the impossible, the outrageous, the unspeakable?"

"We cannot!" exclaimed Molly.

Alfred sighed.

"Then where, at least, do we start?" he said.

"A much more pertinent question," whispered Benjamin. "But first, look there!"

They looked to where he pointed. The silvery edge of the moon had appeared at the city horizon. A church spire and a factory chimney were already silhouetted upon it. A flock of late starlings flickered and danced and swirled across it.

"No time to waste!" yelled Benjamin. "Get the ladder to the roof!"

Alfred shook his head.

"It's too big to get in the lift," he said. "And to carry it so far..."

"Too big! So far!" laughed Benjamin. "Where's your ambition, Alfred?" He cupped his hands to his mouth and called into the sky. "Friends!" he yelled. "Friends and neighbours!" He tried to call again. "I'm losing my voice, sister," he croaked. "All this talking and telling tales after all the years of sacks and silence. We need a boomy voice for this part."

Molly patted his back.

"There, there," she said softly. Then she cleared her throat and turned her face up to the sky.

"Friends and neighbours!" she called. "FRIENDS AND NEIGHBOURS! WE NEED YOUR HELP!"

Nothing happened. Perhaps her voice was deadened by the city's low, constant roar. Perhaps the friends and neighbours were deadened by plates of sausages or the chatter of TV or they lay snoring and catatonic on sofas after their hard day's work. Perhaps her voice simply bounced and echoed off the sheer walls of the apartment block and ricocheted uselessly upwards into the endless night sky.

Molly yelled again. "FRIENDS AND NEIGHBOURS! FRIENDS AND NEIGH-BOURS!"

Still nothing. No answer. No face at a window.

"We should all shout together," said Paul.

"Obvious," said Benjamin. "But also true."

So they yelled together, croaky Benjamin, young Paul, Alfred and Francesca and boomy Molly.

"FRIENDS AND NEIGHBOURS."

"FRIENDS AND NEIGHBOURS."

"FRIENDS AND NEIGHBOURS!"

"FRIENDS AND NEIGHBOURS!"

"FRIENDS
AND
NEIGHBOURS!"

At last a face appeared at a window on Floor 4. Then another on Floor 7. They kept calling. More faces came. Windows inched open. The moon continued to rise, a great high bright dome over the horizon.

"I AM MOLLY!" yelled Molly. "I AM THE IDENTICAL TWIN SISTER OF MABEL, ARTIST AND NEIGHBOUR WHO LIVES AT THE TOP BUT WHO IS CURRENTLY CRUISING DOWN THE NILE! THESE ARE MY FAMILY AND FRIENDS. WE ARE ENGAGED IN A GREAT AND OUTRAGEOUS EXPEDITION! WE NEED YOUR HELP! WE NEED TO GET ALFRED'S LADDER TO THE ROOF!"

"But what can we do?" came a voice, tumbling down from the heights.

"STICK YOUR HANDS OUT OF THE WINDOW!" yelled Molly. "LIFT THE LADDER."

Hundreds of pale hands appeared, shining in the moonlight, sticking out into the night sky.

"Now give them the ladder," said Molly.

Alfred extended the ladder. He carried it towards the apartment block. The hands took hold of the rungs.

"TAKE IT UP!" called Molly, and the hands began to move from rung to rung, just like they were climbing, but it was the ladder that climbed, foot by foot, window by window, floor by floor, towards the sky.

"To the lift!" said Benjamin.

And they rushed inside and to the lift and pressed button 29 and the doors opened and there was the little man inside. He was standing to attention now. He saluted.

"Good evening," he said. "May I ask what is the purpose of your journey?"

"Oh, do be quiet, Tom," said Molly, and she pushed her way inside.

10

Tom had a black helmet on his head and a clipboard in his hand.

"Madam," he stated, "I can be silent no longer. I am simply doing my duty. We cannot have lifts going up and down all day and all night without a proper process of inspection and assessment."

He took a pen from behind his ear.

"Now," he said. "I see you are heading for Floor 29. What is the purpose of your journey? Is it business or pleasure?"

Molly clicked her tongue. She stamped her feet.

"Both!" she snapped.

"I can tick only one box, madam."

"Business!"

He ticked a box.

"And would you say you use this lift very regularly, regularly, irregularly, very irregularly or not at all?"

"Not at all!" said Molly.

He ticked a box. Paul stared at him.

"And you, young sir," said Tom, "how would you rate your overall lift experience? Are you

76

delirious, pleased, neutral, displeased or totally
cheesed off?"

"Pleased," said Paul.

"No more than pleased?"

"Delirious, then," said Paul.

"Excellent."

Tom ticked a box. The lift rattled and swayed
as it rose. Paul thought of the ladder rising outside.
What if it fell? What if there weren't enough hands
to carry it to the top? What if…

"And how likely are you to use the lift again?" said Tom. "Very likely, likely, neutral, unlikely or extremely unlikely?"

"I will use it again," said Paul.

"Be precise, young sir. Do you mean likely or very likely?"

"Very likely."

"Thank you. And do you prefer to travel upwards or downwards or are you happiest when stationary?"

"Upwards."

"Thank you. And how would you say this lift compares with other lifts in your experience? Much better than, better than, just as good as, worse than or much worse than?"

Paul didn't really have a clue, but he was quite enjoying himself by now.

"Much better than," he said.

"Thank you. And have you any suggestions for lift improvements?"

Paul pondered. It would be quite nice to have a TV in here, or a little pool table, or some books and comics.

"Make it faster," said Benjamin.

"I will certainly put that into my report," said Tom. "But speed can only be relative to the demands of safety, the laws of gravity, the capacity of the lift, the occupancy of the lift, the strength of its engines, the current air pressure, the—"

"Who *are* you?" said Francesca.

"My name is Tom, madam," said Tom. "I am the lift inspector. I inspect, investigate, correlate, calculate and advise."

"Advise who?" said Francesca.

"Anyone with any connection to the lift."

"Like us, you mean?"

"Indeed."

"So what *do* you advise?"

Tom smiled.

"Oh, it's early days, madam. My final report will not be ready for several years. In the meantime, I ask questions, gather facts, get a grasp of the overall picture. Any advice, after all, must be based on the soundest of evidence. Now, may I ask, what is your final destination?"

"The moon," said Benjamin.

Tom wrote, *The moon.*

"And," he said, "would you recommend the use of this lift to your friends?"

"Yes," said Paul.

"Excellent," said Tom.

The lift slowed as it approached Floor 29.

"Thank you for taking part in this survey," said Tom. "And a final question. How would you rate my dealings with the public? Have I been extremely charming, polite, neutral, rather irritating or a total pain in the neck?"

"A total pain the neck," said Benjamin.

"Thank you, sir," said Tom. "Glad to be of service." He stood by the door as it opened. "Be sure to enjoy the rest of your journey."

11

The moon had risen further. It

hung at the centre of the window. It hung over the
horizon, over the glittering city. It inched towards
the apartment block.

The tips of the ladder appeared at the window.
Then a rung, and another rung, and another
rung.

"To the roof!" yelled Benjamin.

Molly opened the apartment door. She reached
down as they stepped into the apartment. There
was a postcard on the floor with a picture of Mount
Fuji on it.

"'Having a lovely time in Japan,'"
she read aloud. "'Wish you were here.
Sayonara. Mabel.'"

"Japan?" gasped Alfred.

"Tectonic plates," said Molly.

Benjamin grabbed a kitchen
chair. He stood on it, reached up
to the trapdoor, and pushed and
rattled and shoved. The trapdoor
opened with a click and a clack,
and dropped open, and there

they were: the night, the stars, the universe. They goggled at the wonder of it. Benjamin grabbed Paul by the waist and lifted him. Francesca gasped in fright.

"Don't worry," said Benjamin. "A boy like this can't fall – not with ideas like his and love like yours."

He lifted Paul higher, and Paul squirmed through onto the roof and he stood up tall and he felt the fresh fizzy breezy sky upon him. He danced and waved his arms.

"Magnificent!" he yelled. "Magnificent! Magnificent! Magnificent!"

Benjamin climbed out after him. They rushed to the edge of the roof. There was the tip of the ladder, trembling as it rose higher and higher. There were the pale, moonlit helping hands sticking out of the windows.

"Keep lifting, friends and neighbours!" called Benjamin.

There was the immense, dizzying wall of the apartment block and the lock-ups below and the pavements and streets and gardens. And now there were people, pouring out from the door of the block and gathering below to look upwards, to see what was happening on the roof of their apartment block as the moon crept across the sky.

"This is a very special boy!" yelled Benjamin. "He has a very special theory!"

"What theory?" shouted somebody.

"That the moon is not the moon but is a great hole in the sky!"

He caught a rung of the ladder. He lifted it higher. There was muttering and jabbering and quarrelling far below.

"Where did he get an idea like that from?" somebody yelled.

"It just came out of my mouth!" yelled Paul.

"Well, put it back in!" yelled somebody.

"You're a crackpot!" yelled somebody else.

"You're a genius!" said another.

"You got any other ideas?" somebody called.

Paul gulped. Suddenly, he couldn't answer. He was just Paul, the lonely boy from the basement.

"Come on! There must be something else!"

Benjamin kicked him gently.

"Oa o!" he said. "Ay u-in!"

Go on! Paul translated. *Say something!*

"Oo i!"

Do it!

"I u oa ay u-in I o-in a oo u ar-in."

Paul stared at Benjamin. He had no idea what it meant. Suddenly Molly was there, climbing through the trapdoor.

"He said, 'If you don't say something, I'm going back to the garden!' So say something quick!"

"U o!" said Benjamin.

The whole ladder was here now. Benjamin tottered as he stepped backwards. The ladder teetered high above him. He glared at Paul. *Say something!*

"Sausages are better than war!" yelled Paul.

"What's that?" someone replied.

"SAUSAGES ARE BETTER THAN WAR!"

"No, they're not!" someone replied.

"YES, THEY ARE!" Paul yelled. "SAU-SAGES ARE MUCH, MUCH BETTER THAN WAR."

"Well said," said Albert and Francesca, climbing out onto the roof.

"He's right!" came another voice from below. "How can we deny it?"

"He's bonkers!" came a call.

"He's a madman! Lock him up!"

"He's a hero!"

"But I'm just the boy from the basement called Paul!" called Paul.

"The moon!" yelled Benjamin. "Here it comes! Paul! Get ready! Molly! Alfred! Francesca! Get ready to hold the ladder tight!"

They stood in a circle and gripped the ladder. It jutted high into the sky.

"Are you ready, Paul?" said Benjamin.

"Yes," said Paul.

And he stepped onto the bottom rung and got ready to climb.

12

It seemed to take an age. The whole world seemed to hold its breath. The moon came closer. It grew. Its silver light poured down on them. The ladder trembled. Then at last the moon was almost right above them. It seemed to fill the sky.

"Now," said Benjamin.

They let the ladder tilt to meet the moon. And the tips of the ladder came to rest on the rim, where the edge of silver met the edge of night.

"Off you go!" Benjamin breathed into Paul's ear.

Paul looked into his mum's eyes, into his dad's eyes.

"Go on, son," they said. "Off you go. We're holding tight."

Paul climbed away from them. One rung, then another, then another. He climbed across the sky, through the shining night, towards the moon.

"Don't look down!" called Molly, but he smiled and looked down anyway, and he saw the magnificent world spread out below him, the city spreading away into the distance, the darkness of the countryside all around, the black bulges of distant mountains, the shining slick of the distant sea. He looked down at the hushed moonlit crowd outside the apartment block, at his family and friends supporting him.

And he waved and climbed again, and climbed again, and at last he came to the great moon. He reached out to touch it, and there was nothing solid there, just a great big circle of brilliant light.

He smiled and sighed.

"Yes!" he whispered. "I was right. The moon is not the moon. It is a lovely hole in the sky."

He stepped further.

"I'm Paul," he whispered. "I'm the boy from the basement."

He paused for a moment.

"Be careful!" called his mum.

"What can you see?" yelled Benjamin.

Paul took no notice.

"I'm the boy who climbed into the moon," he whispered to himself.

And so he climbed into the moon.

13

He sat on the edge. At his back were the night, the world, the universe, going on forever. In front of him just endless silvery light. His legs dangled down into it.

"What can you *see*?" yelled Benjamin.

"Nothing!" answered Paul.

"No bombers?"

"No!"

"That's enough now!" called his mum. "Time to come back down!"

"The moon's moving on!" called his dad.

"Did you come from a cannon, too?" whispered someone.

"Pardon?" whispered Paul into the light.

"Did you? Did you come from a cannon, too?"

Paul widened his eyes. He stared. He saw nothing.

"Jump down," the someone whispered. "Go on. Be brave. Jump down."

Paul looked down past his feet: nothing to be seen down there but endless silvery light.

"Nothing will happen," said the voice. "You will be safe. Be brave."

"Who are you?" he asked.

"I am Fortuna. Jump down."

Do I dare? Paul asked himself. All day he had been getting braver and braver. All day he had been turning from Paul, the rather lonely boy in the basement, into a very different kind of Paul.

"My name is Paul," he said.

"Go on, then, Paul," whispered Fortuna. "Be brave and jump."

And so he jumped, and behind him voices screamed, and he was ready to fall and fall and fall and fall, but he fell hardly any distance at all.

"Well done!"

There was a girl at his side. She took his hand and helped him stand up. She was dark-haired and dark-faced and she wore white satin clothes with silver stars and golden comets and golden moons on them.

"I said," she said, "did you come from a cannon, too?"

"A cannon?" said Paul. "No. I climbed a ladder."

Fortuna raised her eyebrows.

"A *ladder*," she said. "How interesting." She paused and listened to the voices calling from outside the moon. "Who is that calling for you?"

"My mum," said Paul.

"Your *mum*?" She listened to Paul's mum's voice, which was so full of fear and yearning.

"She sounds nice," she said.

"She is," said Paul, and he thought how scared his mum would be, just like she was when he left the basement this morning. *Perhaps I should go back right this minute*, he thought to himself.

"Have you heard of me, Paul?" said Fortuna. "Am I remembered?"

"I don't know," said Paul.

"You don't know!"

"No."

"But wasn't my great catastrophe in all the news?"

Paul didn't know what to say. He knew of many catastrophes, just like everyone on Earth did. But what was Fortuna's catastrophe?

Fortuna frowned.

"Do you mean that while I am here deep inside the moon, back on Earth I am forgotten?"

Paul searched his mind for an answer.

"Well?" she demanded.

"I don't know…" he muttered at last.

"You don't know very much, do you?" she snapped.

"I suppose I don't," admitted Paul.

"I," declared Fortuna, "am Fortuna, the Human Cannonball! I have been blasted from my uncle's cannon across the Hudson River. I have been blasted over Notre Dame. By the time I was eight years old I had flown through the air over the Temple of Baal in Palmyra, over the Kremlin, the Taj Mahal, the Royal Gardens at Kew, the Pump Rooms at Bath, Niagara Falls, the splendid castles of Dunstanburgh and Neufchâtel. And you say I am forgotten!"

Paul shrugged.

"I don't know," he said. "I have to admit that I for one have never heard of you."

"Then you must have led a very sheltered life!"

Paul lowered his eyes.

"I have," he admitted quietly. "Perhaps my friends will remember you, though."

"Ha! Your friends!"

"Yes. Benjamin and Molly and Clara and—"

"Enough of them! They sound like a dreadfully stupid lot!"

"No, they're not. They're very clever. And Benjamin knew a bomber that flew into the moon."

"A bomber! The moon is full of silly bombers and their silly pilots and their silly bombs!"

"Is it?"

"Yes!"

"But doesn't that make the place dangerous?"

"Of course it doesn't! We throw them out, the bombs, that is. Off they go, far out into space. And the pilots soon settle down to life in the moon. Much more peaceful than in your silly world. Huh. Dangerous!"

Paul was silent. He glanced back. He sighed. He could see the tips of the ladder at the edge of the moon. He saw hands reaching up to the tips. He saw Benjamin's pale face appear. He saw Benjamin peer into the light. But like Paul, he clearly could see nothing but the light.

"Who on earth is that?" said Fortuna.

"My friend Benjamin," said Paul.

"Paul!" called Benjamin.

"I'm here, Benjamin!" Paul answered. "I'm all right. I'm safe! I'll be back any minute!"

"The moon is moving on!" said Benjamin. "It will move beyond the ladder's reach."

"Ha!" Fortuna laughed. "And then you'll be lost forever in the moon."

"Like you?" asked Paul.

"Huh. Like me!"

Paul stared at her.

"How did you get here?" he said.

Fortuna took a deep breath.

"It was early evening," she said. "Everything was prepared. The huge cannon pointed towards the stars.

There in front of us
was the Great Pyramid.
Beyond it was the great net
waiting to catch me. And the crowds,
hundreds of people, thousands of people, all
waiting in the warm still night to see a girl – me!
The Great Fortuna! – bulleting across the sky, to
see *me* speeding through the shining night across
the ancient pyramid to yet more glory. Cameras
everywhere, reporters everywhere. Fans cheering,
drums drumming. '*For-tun-a! For-tun-a! For-tun-
a!*' It is all prepared. Uncle puts the silver helmet
on my head and kisses me. 'I have put in an extra
pinch of gunpowder, my girl,' he whispers. Ha! His
last words to me – 'I have put in an extra pinch of
gunpowder. It will do no harm, my niece.' Ha! I
climb up the ladder, I wave, I slide down into the
great barrel, as I have a hundred times before. I
look up to the perfect ring through which I will

be launched. I see the edge of the moon. I hear the final drumroll, the blast of a trumpet. Then BANG! WALLOP! WHOOSH! Out I fly, straight across the pyramid, and straight into the moon."

"Golly!" said Paul. "That must have hurt."

"No more than usual. And one must suffer for one's art."

"And your uncle must be bereft."

"Must he? I have a cousin, a silly thing called Florella. He will have trained her up."

"And what did your parents think of it all?"

"Ha! They had been taken, long ago." She stamped and grunted. "Ha! That's enough of that! Quite enough!" She stamped again, then closed her eyes for a moment and hummed a gentle tune. "There! I have decided to be nicer to you now. Would you like to meet some others?"

"I should go back," said Paul.

"But you've just arrived, and you've much more time than that silly Benjamin seems to think. Come on. Be brave for once in your life."

"What do you mean, for once in my life? I've been brave all day long."

"Huh! All day long. Prove it, then. This way, Mr Brave Boy."

So Paul allowed her to lead him deeper into the light.

14

"They've been coming in since time began," said Fortuna.

"What have?" said Paul.

"The things that fly, of course. It is commonly thought that the moon is a solid thing—"

"Not by me," interrupted Paul.

"No?" said Fortuna. "Then there's something like a brain inside that silly skull of yours. Anyway, first of all there were lifeless things – meteors and meteorites and asteroids and comets. Then came pterodactyls and the archaeopteryx, and bats and owls, and midges and mosquitoes, and eagles, swallows, swifts, skylarks, homing pigeons, migrating geese, dragonflies, flying squirrels, flying foxes. Choose the right evening to fly high and in they go, straight into the moon."

"And they're still here?" said Paul.

"And many are still here. And there are javelins and arrows and spears and boomcrangs, and boulders from ancient catapults, and footballs and cricket balls and baseballs, and bullets and shells and bigger shells and bombers like your silly friend's bomber and even bigger shells and bombs and bigger bombs. And hot-air balloons. And biplanes, triplanes, gliders, hang gliders, zeppelins, airships, helicopters, jets, faster jets, more of your bombers, bigger bombers, even faster jets and even bigger bombers and their even bigger bigger bombs. And missiles and anti-missile missiles, and anti-missile-missile missiles. And—"

"But how do they all fit in?" gasped Paul.

Fortuna smiled.

"That," she answered, "is one of the mysteries of the moon. And pilots and trapeze artists and astronauts and beautiful mad folk who dedicated their lives to learning to fly like birds, and one or two like me blasted out from the barrels of great cannons. And beings you would not believe. And … and boys like you who climb! And they are nice people, most of them, even those that press the buttons to blast the missiles and drop the bombs. A week or two in the moon and they revert to being good, kind people again, just like all of us can be. Huh! Maybe everybody down on Earth should be made to spend a year up here in the moon. That'd get things sorted out. Now, halt a moment while I find my bearings."

She stood still. She stared forwards into the light. She waved her hand before her eyes as if clearing away a haze.

"And people leave, of course," murmured Fortuna. "That helps to keep the numbers down."

"They leave?"

"Of course they do. They go out on the Great Expeditions."

"But where to?"

"My goodness," said Fortuna. "Where on earth do you think they go to? Have you no imagination in you?"

"Yes," said Paul.

"Then use it!"

He tried to use it. But he still couldn't think of an answer.

"Now," said Fortuna, "if you can't use your imagination, use your eyes and look."

"Look where?"

"Straight in front of you, of course."

Paul peered.

"But there's nothing," he whispered. And then, "Oh, golly! Yes, there is!"

15

A pair of multicoloured hot-air balloons drifted high above. People peered over the sides of the baskets. They called out to Fortuna. They waved and smiled and she waved back. Further off, a helicopter spun into view with its blades clattering. And now there were drifting parachutists and hang gliders and soaring birds. A meteorite whooshed past far, far above. And then a great beaked scaly creature appeared, with heavily beating wings. Paul's mouth dropped open.

"Pterodactyl," said Fortuna. "As I told you. You will see many more if you decide to stay. Don't dawdle. Come on."

Paul rubbed his eyes and followed. A couple of astronauts walked by, wearing astronaut suits, deep in conversation.

"Hello, Fortuna!" they called.

"Hello!" she answered.

Paul watched as they walked on.

"They're from the mission to Mars that disappeared," whispered Fortuna. She looked at him. She stamped her feet and shook her head. "You don't even remember *that*, do you?"

"Paul!" came a voice from very far away.

"Your mum," said Fortuna.

She turned and gazed back towards the dark circle.

"Oh, look!" she whispered.

Paul looked back. Now his mum was with Benjamin, teetering at the top of the ladder and gripping the rim of the moon and goggling into the light.

"That's her?" said Fortuna.

"Yes," said Paul.

"Oh, she looks very pretty."

"She is. I really can't stay. I really have to go."

Fortuna took his hand.

"Five more minutes," she said. She led him forwards. "Just a little further."

"Paul!" his mum yelled.

Fortuna turned to look again.

"Is she *nice*?" asked Fortuna.

"Oh, yes," said Paul. "And so's my dad."

"Your *dad*? You have a *dad*?"

"Yes. He's called Alfred. He's a window cleaner."

Fortuna sighed.

"Oh, a mum," she whispered. "*And* a dad!"

And as they looked back, Paul's dad appeared too.

Fortuna sighed.

"Where are *your* parents?" asked Paul.

That made Fortuna grunt and stamp her feet again.

"They were taken! I told you that!"

"What do you mean, taken?"

"They died, you stupid boy!"

"Oh."

Paul stood still. He was so ashamed.

"I'm so stupid," he whispered. "I'm so sorry."

"So you should be!" she snapped. Then she calmed again. "Never mind. It can't be helped, not even up here in the moon. Come on. I'll show you a little bit more, then you can climb down your ladder again with your precious parents and your silly friend, and you can put us all out of your little mind."

She led him forwards. They passed a small mountain of heaped-up helicopters, aeroplanes and rockets. They came upon a group of people – including pilots in pilot helmets, a man wearing home-made wings, a woman in a shimmering trapeze-artist costume – crouched intently around some kind of map showing spheres amid great tracts of tiny stars and utter darkness.

"They're planning a Great Expedition," whispered Fortuna.

"Oh," said Paul.

He didn't dare ask where to. He watched the people's fingers tracing pathways through the universe. They murmured together of great distances, great tracts of time, the need to prepare properly for departure. Paul could be silent no longer.

"Where will you go to?" he asked.

Fortuna clicked her tongue.

"Don't interrupt, silly boy!" she said.

But a pilot turned to him and smiled.

"We have looked into the sky," he said. "We have looked at Venus."

The trapeze artist turned to him.

"We have concluded that Venus is not Venus," she said.

Paul gasped.

"It is a great hole in the sky!" he said.

The winged man turned. His feathers rustled.

"Yes," he said. "And the purpose of our Great Expedition is to enter Venus."

"Golly," said Paul. "You're just like me!"

He grinned. He looked at the pilots.

"My name is Paul," he said. "Can I ask – was one of you a bomber pilot?"

"I was," said a pilot wearing a dark green uniform with an eagle on its pocket.

"Were you about to drop some bombs when you disappeared into the moon?"

"I was," said the pilot.

"My friend Benjamin saw you," continued Paul. "One moment you were there, the next…"

"Yes," said the pilot. "That was me, in an old sad life. Now I am transfigured."

"Benjamin told me about you, just today."

"Then I am remembered?"

"Yes. You are." Paul smiled. "Sausages are better than war."

"Yes. Most things, including sausages, are far better than any war."

The bomber turned back to the charts.

"I climbed here on a ladder," said Paul. "I climbed right across the sky."

"Then you are indeed like us," said the trapeze artist.

With her finger she traced the shape of an imaginary ladder stretching all the way from the opening of the moon to the opening of Venus.

"There," she said. "That is what we intend, Paul. A great and splendid ladder. We will make it, and we will climb together into Venus."

Paul's heart thumped with joy at the idea of it.

"Maybe you could help us, Paul," said the bomber pilot. "Maybe you could climb with us all the way to Venus."

"Paul!" yelled his mum. "Paul! Paul!"

Paul and Fortuna turned together.

"His mum," said Fortuna. "She's nice, and also pretty."

"The moon is moving on!" yelled Benjamin.

"I have to go home," said Paul.

"Then go," said the trapeze artist. "But keep us in mind, Paul. And watch out for us, climbing our ladder across the sky."

"Paul!" yelled Paul's mum. "Paul!"

"Go on, Paul," said the winged man. "Hurry home or stay forever."

"Good-bye!" said Paul quickly. "I will remember you all. Good-bye."

He started to hurry towards his mum's voice. Fortuna kept at his side.

"Look!" she said as a creature flew in from the night and headed towards them.

"It's Clarence!" laughed Paul.

The poodle flew towards them. He looked very smart in his clipped white coat and his neat red jacket. There was a badge pinned on him. I AM 7.

"Happy birthday, Clarence!" said Paul.

"Thank you," said Clarence. "I have come to inform you that the moon is moving onwards. Soon the ladder will fall away. Your mother is bereft. Benjamin is calm. He says that a boy like you will certainly find his way back to the ladder in time. But I urge you. Hurry! Yap!"

"You're a talking poodle!" said Fortuna.

"That is correct," said Clarence. "My name is Clarence. It is my seventh birthday and my strange ideas have been proven to be right. Yap! Run, Paul! Run!"

Paul ran. Fortuna ran at his side.

"Maybe I'll come back again some night," he said. "Maybe I'll see you again."

"Yes," she gasped.

"I'm coming back!" yelled Paul. "Reach down into the light, Dad. Get ready to pull me up!"

"At last!" called his mum.

"Clear the way!" shouted Clarence. "Mums and Benjamins to the foot of the ladder, please."

Paul's mum and Benjamin descended. His dad reached out. Paul and Fortuna approached the dark exit from the moon. It was just like a dark moon itself. It was just like the barrel of a cannon. It was just like an opening in the mind.

"I'm here!" yelled Paul.

He jumped for his dad's hand. He couldn't reach it. He jumped again. He couldn't reach.

"A little to the left!" called Clarence. "And lean a little further if you could, sir."

At last Paul jumped and caught his dad's hand. He clung to it. He dangled for a moment as his dad began to pull him up.

"Take me with you," said Fortuna.

"Pardon?"

"Take me with you, down your ladder, back into the world."

He looked into her dark face, her dark eyes.

"Can I?" he said.

"Of course. The strangest things are possible when boys climb out from basements, when poodles talk and fly, when we find out that the moon is not the moon."

"I will!" said Paul.

He was lifted by his dad up to the rim. They hugged each other tight. Then Paul turned back and reached down into the brilliant light. He felt Fortuna's hand in his. He lifted her and they saw her dark face, her dark hair, her dark eyes emerging from the light.

She clambered up beside them.

"This is Fortuna," said Paul. "My friend from inside the moon."

They sat for a moment alongside Paul's dad with their backs against the light and their feet dangling down into the dark. There below were his mum and Molly and Benjamin holding the ladder. Close behind them were Harry and Clara. There was the apartment block and the crowd around it, and the town and the curving world.

"I'd forgotten!" gasped Fortuna, "It's all so, so…"

"Magnificent," said Paul.

"Yes, magnificent," said Fortuna.

So they climbed down, and as they climbed, the moon moved on and the tips of the ladder rested on nothing, just darkness. They stepped down onto the roof of the apartment block. There was a great cheer from the crowd below. Paul's mum grasped him to her breast.

"Hug my friend as well," he said. "This is Fortuna, my friend from inside the moon."

Harry hooted with delight. He sprinted on the spot.

"What a marvel that lad is!" he said. "Every time I come across him, there he is with yet another pal. Is there no end to your gregariousness, lad?"

Paul smiled and looked down.

"No," said his mum. "There is not."

She kissed Fortuna's cheek.

"Hello, love," she said.

"Hello," whispered Fortuna, suddenly shy.

"I or a o-i a-i," said Benjamin.

"Pardon?" said Paul.

"Sausage sandwich!" called out Clarence, flying down. "He said it's time for a sausage sandwich."

16

They climbed down through the trapdoor and dropped to the floor of Molly's apartment. Molly fried sausages and cut bread and made sandwiches and put them on the table. Everybody ate. The moon drifted away through the magnificent night.

Clarence swooped and tumbled through the air around their heads. He sang "O for the Wings of a Dove" in the sweetest of voices. Clara sighed and watched him proudly.

"Clarence," she said, "you are indeed an exemplary poodle."

"Thank you, my dear," said Clarence.

Harry jogged on the spot as he munched. He kept looking towards the door, desperate to get sprinting again.

Fortuna sat between Paul and his mum. She ate slowly and timidly, but her shyness faded. She relaxed and smiled. She began to murmur her memories of the moon, of pterodactyls and bombers and hang gliders and splendid light.

"It sounds lovely," Paul's mum whispered.

"It was," said Fortuna. "But it's better to be back here in the world again."

"Tell them about the night beside the pyramid," said Paul.

Fortuna smiled.

"It was early evening," she said. "Everything was prepared. The huge silver cannon—"

"Hang on!" said Molly. "I knew you reminded me of something!"

She trotted across the room to a cupboard. She took a big book out of it. She slapped it onto the table. It was called *A History of the Great Cannonball Acts.* She turned the pages.

"There!" she said.

Everyone leaned close. They saw a photograph,

taken at evening. There was the Great Pyramid, a full moon, and a cannon with smoke belching from its barrel. And high above it, a tiny white figure streaked into the sky.

"Me!" gasped Fortuna.

"You!" said Molly.

She read the words beneath: *The last sighting of the Great Fortuna, who disappeared into the desert night.*

"Did you hear?" said Fortuna. "The Great Fortuna. The *Great* Fortuna."

Paul's mum hugged her.

"Then I am remembered," said Fortuna.

"Yes, you are, love," said Paul's mum. "And here you are among us in a brand-new family in a brand-new life."

Fortuna blushed.

"Thanks to Paul," she said.

"And his crackpot notions," said Benjamin. "And his courage."

Paul smiled. He looked out at the retreating moon. He imagined the great ladder reaching towards Venus. He imagined climbing it, rung by rung by rung.

Then the doorbell rang, and Molly ran to open the door.

"It's Mabel!" she cried.

In stepped Mabel. She looked just like Molly,
but with a suntan and with a rucksack on her back.

"I just popped in on my way to Caracas," she
said.

Then she stopped. She goggled at everybody.

"What lovely people!" she said.

She dashed to a cupboard. She took out some paints and brushes and an easel.

"Oh!" she cried. "What a beautiful picture you'll make!"

David Almond is known worldwide as the Carnegie, Whitbread and Smarties award-winning author of *Skellig*, *The Fire-Eaters* and many other novels, stories and plays. *The Boy Who Climbed into the Moon* is his third novel for younger readers, following *My Dad's a Birdman*, also illustrated by Polly Dunbar, and *The Savage* – an extraordinary part novel, part graphic-novel illustrated by Dave McKean.

David grew up in a big, busy family in a coal-mining town on the river Tyne, where stories were part of life. "I always knew I'd be a writer – I wrote stories and stitched them into little books. I had aunts and uncles who could have a room of folk in fits of laughter and tears with their tales. I loved our local library and dreamed of seeing books with my name on the covers. I also dreamed of playing for Newcastle United (and I still wait for the call)."

David lives in Northumberland with his family, and writes in a cabin at the bottom of his garden, where he makes tea and is visited by the birds.

"He has the exquisite ability to describe the nature of love and the constant wonder of being alive."
The Whitbread Judges

Polly Dunbar is the winner of the Red House Children's Book Award and one of The Big Picture's top ten Best New Illustrators. She is the author/illustrator of *Dog Blue*, *Flyaway Katie*, *Here's a Little Poem*, *Penguin* and the Tilly and Friends series. She says, "*The Boy Who Climbed into the Moon* was an extraordinary book to illustrate, it has such surreal twists and turns. As the character Paul gains self-belief, he becomes more and more adventurous and wonderful things start to happen! I tried to illustrate this book with the same attitude – anything is possible!"

Polly lives and works in Brighton. She thinks that colour is a brilliant way to cheer yourself up and whenever she's feeling grey, she puts on her best pink frock and paints! When she's not illustrating, she likes to make puppets.

About *My Dad's a Birdman*:
"This beautiful book ... will make children laugh while encouraging them to believe in themselves and others and to tolerate strangeness."
The Sunday Times